The Boston Cream Pirate™

Sam McDowell

Story & Illustrations by Sam McDowell
Written by Rider McDowell

For my children
-Sam McDowell

The Boston Cream Pirate™

Story and Illustrations by Sam McDowell
Written by Rider McDowell
Additional Illustrations by Jeff Moores
Special thanks to Chris Benzel for his masterful graphics and design work.
Copyright 2014 TJR McDowell

Published by Pine Brothers Charity Press
PO Box 492
Pebble Beach, CA 93953

pinebros.com

First Edition.
Printed in China.

ISBN 978-1-4951-1160-0

This is a story about the townsfolk of Boston, which once was so small, it was hard to get lost in. Just a spit of a town, a few hundred acres, but already famous for its famous pie makers. The best-est among them was Lucy McTy, known for her pluck and her Boston Cream Pie. Her pies were renowned for their plump robust flavor. The aroma alone was something to savor.

So on with the story that you'll like a lot, and so we begin and here now the plot.

In a small portside pub in old Boston Harbor, a group of men gathered to hear Captain Farbor. A blustery man with well tended hair, it also transpired that Farbor was mayor. He'd heard that a ship full of pirates was approaching, so he gathered the men folk, it took little coaching. "You see lads, I've heard there are pirates about. Lets get in our ship and kick the bums out!"

But the lady folk worried with no men around, who would remain to protect the town? The ladies were brave and intrepid that's true, but averaged in height less than five feet and two. Plus as was agreed by most everyone, girls fighting pirates, well it just wasn't done. Ladies are tough but sensitive creatures, even back then before ladies wore sneakers.

5.2"

But the men were determined and welcomed the fight, and these men in particular always were right. They had all of the answers, for much of their lives. They knew what was best, why go ask their wives.

4

Farbor gathered the townsfolk right there on the dock, and said they were ready, "This is nothing ad-hoc. We'll capture those cut throats and give 'em what for, throw 'em in irons and lock up the door. We won't linger long, we'll be back in an hour, we'll outflank the pirates with our giant sail power. Just trust me dear townsfolk, no need to despair, and after we've won, I'm re-running for mayor!"

So the men started singing and hip hip hooraying, which sounded to some like donkeys when braying. "It's under control, girls, reign in your alarm. We won't let them scare you or bring you to harm." Farbor bowed to the ladies and patted some heads, and then recommended they get to their beds.

"I certainly hope that they know what they're doing," said Mrs. Von Entress in a tone like poo-pooing. "Cause my husband old Barney, he tells me he's bright, but lately I've wondered if Barney is right. And though we poor ladies lack something in stature, I'd trade you his chances for half a salt cracker."

"Oh, come now, my dears," said old Mrs. Mant. "If they want to fight pirates, who says that they can't. They seem to know everything, that part is true, but that's just their nature, that's what men do. Lets wish them Godspeed and salute their attack, and if they return, we'll welcome them back."

So off the men sailed, their
expressions heroic, as the lady
folk waved, their visages quite
stoic. Some women tried
shouting, but their heart wasn't
in it, until pirates appeared in
less than a minute.

The pirates were waiting,
as they're wont to do, until
the harbor was empty and
authorities few. They sailed
in pell mell, their pirate flag
wavy, exulting and laughing
at the lack of a navy.

"Good gosh," said a voice in old Boston Brahmin,
"The pirates are coming. We've nothing in common.
They'll plunder and pillage and stare at our legs.
They'll make us walk planks and hang us from pegs."

There was panic and bedlam and fear at their coming, and conduct most Boston folk find unbecoming. It seemed they were done for, at the mercy of beasts, except for one woman who cared not in the least. Dear Lucy McTy, she'd concocted a plan, that would vanquish the pirates right down to a man. She went right to her pie shop and turned on the light, and beheld in her kitchen a glorious sight. For you see she'd been up for two days, maybe more, baking her pies which were meant for the store.

Her Boston Cream Pies were the talk of the town, from the east to the west, to the up and the down. She moved 'cross the shop to gaze out the door. The pirates were nearing, just five minutes more! She called to the women folk still on the piers, "Get over here, girls, and dry up those tears!"

The ladies assembled and she shared her plan, and swiftly the lady folk smiled with elan. "It's genius!" "Inspired!" "It's really quite good." "I think it will work," Lucy said knocking wood.

They gathered the wheelbarrows and stood at the door and stacked up the pies while Lucy made more. "Pies are the favorite of men of this ilk, and while we're at it, let's bring them some milk."

"Alright," Lucy beckoned, "It's off to the ship. And remember our manners and stiff upper lip. They may be psychotic, blood thirsty and grumpy, but even with pirates, we won't appear frumpy." They marched to the docks, their little heads high, their wheelbarrows laden with pie after pie.

The pirates stood watching, each scoundrel more seedy, but their eyes saw the pies, and their expressions turned greedy. For everyone knows that pies with this topping, for pirates who eat them, they'll have trouble stopping.

When suddenly leaping high up on the mast, stood the boss of the pirates, who screamed, "Not so fast!" That he was the captain, was instantly clear, from the hook on his hand to the ring in his ear. His leg full of termites, his whiskers with vermin, he shook his hooked hand and said, "I'm Captain Merman!"

"What is it you ladies would like to discuss, for that's why you're here, so just tell it to us." He smiled like a devil and exuded some charm, while assuring them, truly, that he meant no harm.

The pirates beneath him, a treacherous crew, were significantly larger than five feet and two. They grinned and they leered and they bared their brown teeth, then pulled out their swords from their place in their sheath. What the pirates were planning, why, there was no telling, but what was apparent was what they were smelling. For try as they might to put fear in their eyes, they couldn't help staring below at the pies.

"Dear Captain," remarked little Lucy McTy, "Allow us to offer some Boston Cream Pie. We saw you arriving and thought at your leisure, you might enjoy pie before looking for treasure."

"Cor blimey," Captain Merman said, licking his lips. "We've had very few pies while out, pillaging ships. How thoughtful, how kind. How nice and so droll. If your pie ain't no good, why it's right in the hole. I'll keel haul you, hang you, and boil you in oil. Don't matter to me, if you're just a goil (girl!). I'll feed you to sharks and chop you to bits. Now bring up the wheelbarrow, let's see if it fits."

The ladies obliged, one after the other, reminding some pirates of home and their mother. Captain Merman was first to partake of a slice, inhaling it whole then growling out, "Nice! Bring them aboard, aye, come quickly, don't tarry! As many fresh pies as you ladies can carry!"

So they plied them with pies and followed with milk. The ladies encouraged with voices like silk. "Eat up boys, please hurry, no shoving, act fairly. But relish these pies, because you get them so rarely." And being delicious fresh Boston Cream Pies, the pirates had stomachs smaller than their eyes. And just as intended by Lucy McTy, the pirates were helpless to stop eating pie. Her pies gave them comfort, which was almost prenatal, but eating too much, well, that could prove fatal.

The pirates had fallen right into a groove, and soon grew so fat, that they just couldn't move.

The Captain among them was round as a toad, and here comes the punch line of our little ode. Though ladies in general are frailer, that's true, they'd figured out just what their men couldn't do.

They tied up the pirates
and took them to jail.
Each one just as plump
and as stout as a whale.
Who knew that just
pies would prove so
effective. Whoops, there
goes Captain Merman
screaming invective.

And when the good menfolk returned empty handed, the ladies casually said pirates had landed. They poured forth their saga, how the pirates did tumble, and the menfolk looked crestfallen, tired, and humble.

And standing there dully on the edge of the harbor, stood slightly embarrassed, that old Captain Farbor. "I hate to admit it, but our thinking was wrong. We haven't been right for ever so long. And though we're quite happy in our growing nation, perhaps what is called for is wives' liberation. From now on we'll listen, and make some amends. For more than our wives, you're our very best friends."

And later that year, it's now safe to share, Lucy McTy was elected to mayor. And the townsfolk all praised her right through to the skies, for they all loved her pluck and her Boston Cream Pies.

Afterword

Occasionally you hear the expression 'a labor of love,' and this little book is a shining example of that. It was illustrated and written by Sam McDowell for his four children back in 1969 when his children were smaller. They're much bigger now, and last year it occurred to his oldest son Rider to dust off the pages, rewrite the story, and add some new illustrations in the hope that a wider audience of children might enjoy this classic tale. And that's what was done. Sam McDowell (Dad) is older now, as are his children who have grown bigger and have children of their own. We hope you enjoy this little tale of pirates and feminine derring do from our family to yours with love and pie...

R. McDowell
Pebble Beach, CA

Dad

Pirate